SPIRIT WARRIORS™

SPIRIT WARRIORS, Book 1
By Stephen Baldwin & Bruno Rosato

ISBN: 0-8054-4357-6
ISBN-13: 978-0-8054-4357-8

B & H Publishing Group
Nashville, Tennessee

Illustration Team:
Pencils/Character Profiles by Joe Simko
Inking by Jeral Tidwell & David Witt
Cover by Joe Simko & Jeral Tidwell

Dewey Decimal Classification: F
Subject Heading: FANTASY FICTION

1 2 3 4 5   10 09 08 07 06

STEPHEN BALDWIN'S

SPIRIT WARRIORS™

NUMBER
ONE

B&H
PUBLISHING GROUP
NASHVILLE, TENNESSEE

MEET THE
SPIRIT WARRIORS
LIVIN' IT
FIRE WALL
MERC
RISING
ALL AGES
MAY

MIA
Simko

NANO
SMOKE
Simko

FAITH
FAITH
Simko

JON!
Simko

DAVY
Simko

HAILEY
Simko

NEW CITY

NOOOOOOOO
MIA!

VWHOOOM!!!
ARE YOU OK?
EVIL HAS WON.
IT WAS JUST A NIGHTMARE.

THE NEXT MORNING
MORNIN' SIS.
MORNIN' GARY.
YOU GOT TO STOP THIS JESUS STUFF. THAT'S WHY YOU GET NIGHT-MARES.
GET OUT OF THE HOUSE AND DO SOMETHING!
HUH?
IT'S NOT SAFE OUT THERE!

NEITHER IS READING YOUR BIBLE & PRAYING ALL DAY!
YOU SHOULD SPEND MORE TIME READING YOUR BIBLE INSTEAD OF YOUR EGO!
YOU SHOULD BE NICE TO HER.
SHE'S ALMOST BEEN KIDNAPPED TWICE!

Rrrr...

WHOOSH

Guuuu
WHACK

TAP TAP

BAM
ugh
uhg!
ZHWACK!!
CRACK!
UGH!
ohh

MOMMY....

ORD, WHO ARE THEY?"

SCCREEEEEE
SHOOOOOM
BOOM

RD, WHAT ARE THESE VISIONS ABOUT?
UHH . . . SIS?
YOU KNOW I LOVE YOU. . .
AND ALWAYS WILL.
I'VE GOT TO GO TO WORK.
I LOVE YOU TOO . . . THANKS. SEE YOU LATER.

OH YEAH...
SAY HELLO TO
JESUS FOR ME!
SLAM

MY CHILD . . .
My word is true. Put on My full armor, so that when the day of evil comes, you may be able to stand your ground, and after you have done everything to stand. Stand firm then, with the belt of truth buckled around your waist, with the breastplate of righteousness in place, and with your feet fitted with the readiness that comes from the gospel of peace. In addition to all this, take up the shield of faith, against flaming arrows of the evil one. Take the helmet of salvation and the sword of the spirit, which is My word. And pray in the spirit on all occasions with all kinds of prayers and requests. With this in mind, be alert and always keep on praying. You are chosen to bring back the goodness to New City.

BUT GOD, WHY ME?

WELL DONE! SIX REMAIN. WE WILL BRING FREEDOM AND LIFE TO THIS TOWN.

BUT WHY WOULD HE WANT ME TO FIGHT EVIL? I'M AFRAID OF MY OWN SHADOW.
IT'S ALL PART OF HIS PLAN
12
3
6
9
IMPOSSIBLE, ME?
IT'S NINE O'CLOCK, WHERE'S GARY?

MAYBE HE'S STILL AT WORK. I'LL TRY TO CALL HIM
BEEP
BEEP
BEEP
TURILLO'S PIZZA
YES, HELLO. IS GARY THERE?
TURILLO'S PIZZA
PIZZA
HE LEFT TWO HOURS AGO.

TWO HOURS AGO!
YEP.

GUITAR
ROCK N ROLL
STORY OF ATOMS

I'VE CALLED EVERY-WHERE, NOBODY HAS SEEN HIM...
I HAVE TO GO FIND HIM.
I'M COMING WITH YOU!
AND I'M READY FOR ANYTHING.

HNNNNNN
I'M READY FOR ANYTHING, NNNNNN!
NNNNN...
YAAAAA
OW.

WHY ME GOD? PLEASE HELP.
POLICE

gulp!

YAAAA
KOOF

WHACK!
POW!
THESE ARE THE KIDS FROM MY DREAM!
UH. . . THANKS. . .
PLEASED TO MEET YOU. I'M DAVY, THE MOST WANTED KID IN THE CITY. . . WELL MAYBE AFTER YOU.
THIS IS MY SISTER, HAILEY.

From a distance a charismatic preacher brings a message that is refreshing in the middle of New City; a city painted in immorality.
ALL GATHER
LIES
THEY'VE TAKEN US
END IS NEA
LIES

ONLY JESUS WILL SAVE YOU. HE IS THE WAY, THE TRUTH & THE LIFE . . . JESUS IS HERE, JESUS IS THERE, JESUS IS EVERY-WHERE . . . IT IS UP TO YOU. IF YOU WANT TO FIND HIM . . . I CAN SHOW YOU THE WAY TO HIM . . . FOLLOW ME . . . FOLLOW ME... FOLLOW ME . . . TO THE PROMISED LAND CHURCH TONIGHT . . . 6PM TONIGHT
THAT VOICE SOUNDS SO FAMILIAR.
THAT'S IT!
LIGHT HOUSE ORPHANAGE

PASTOR PROMISE, IT'S ME, MIA.
OH DEAR GOD. . IT'S BEEN SO LONG. HOW ARE YOU?
WHY IT SEEMS LIKE ONLY YESTERDAY . . . I WAS THINKING OF YOU

AND SO . . .
The kids enter the city. Poverty, graffiti, sex, gangs, hatred. What a dirty place New City has become.

WHOA!

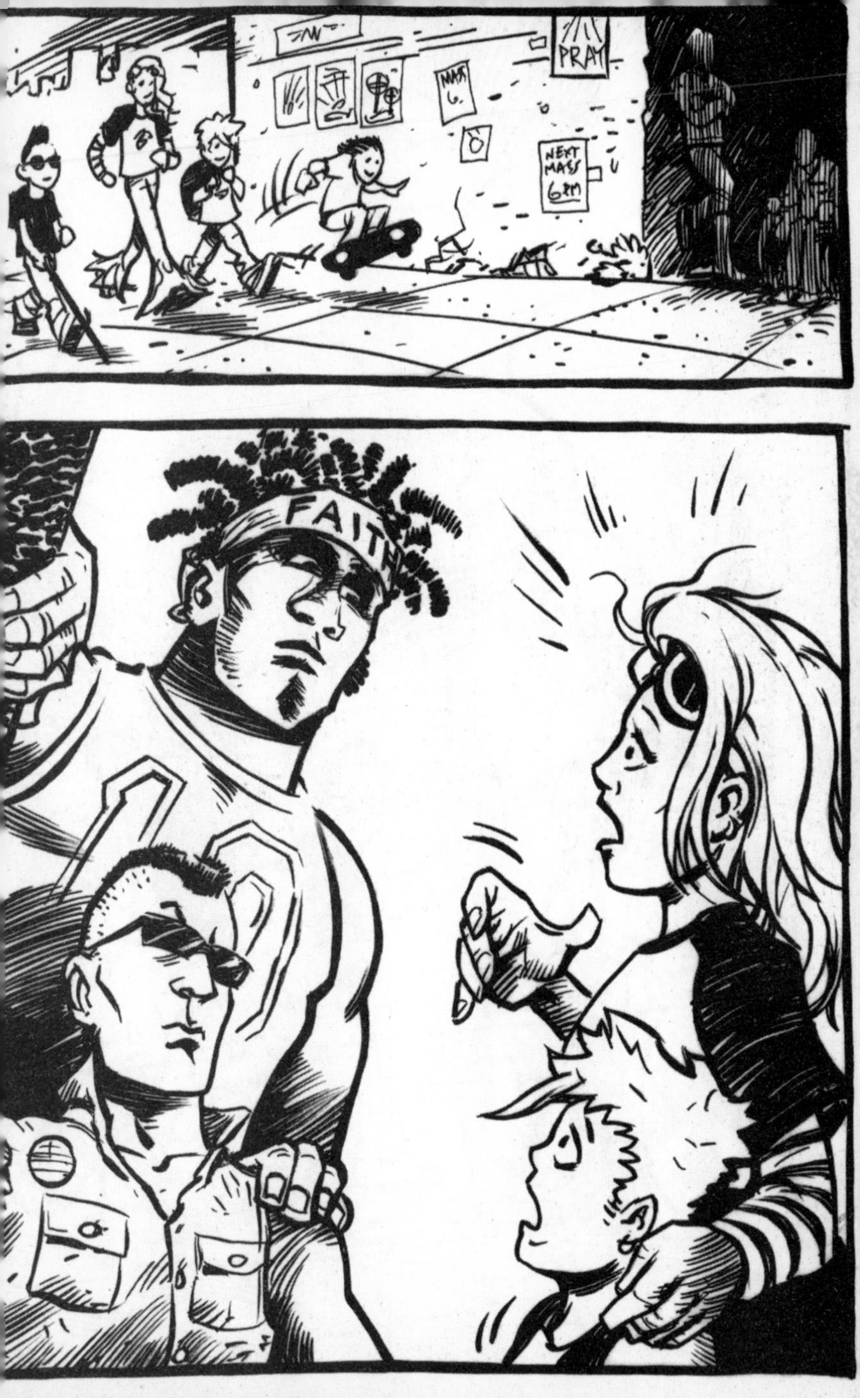
PRAY
NEXT MASS 6PM
FAITH

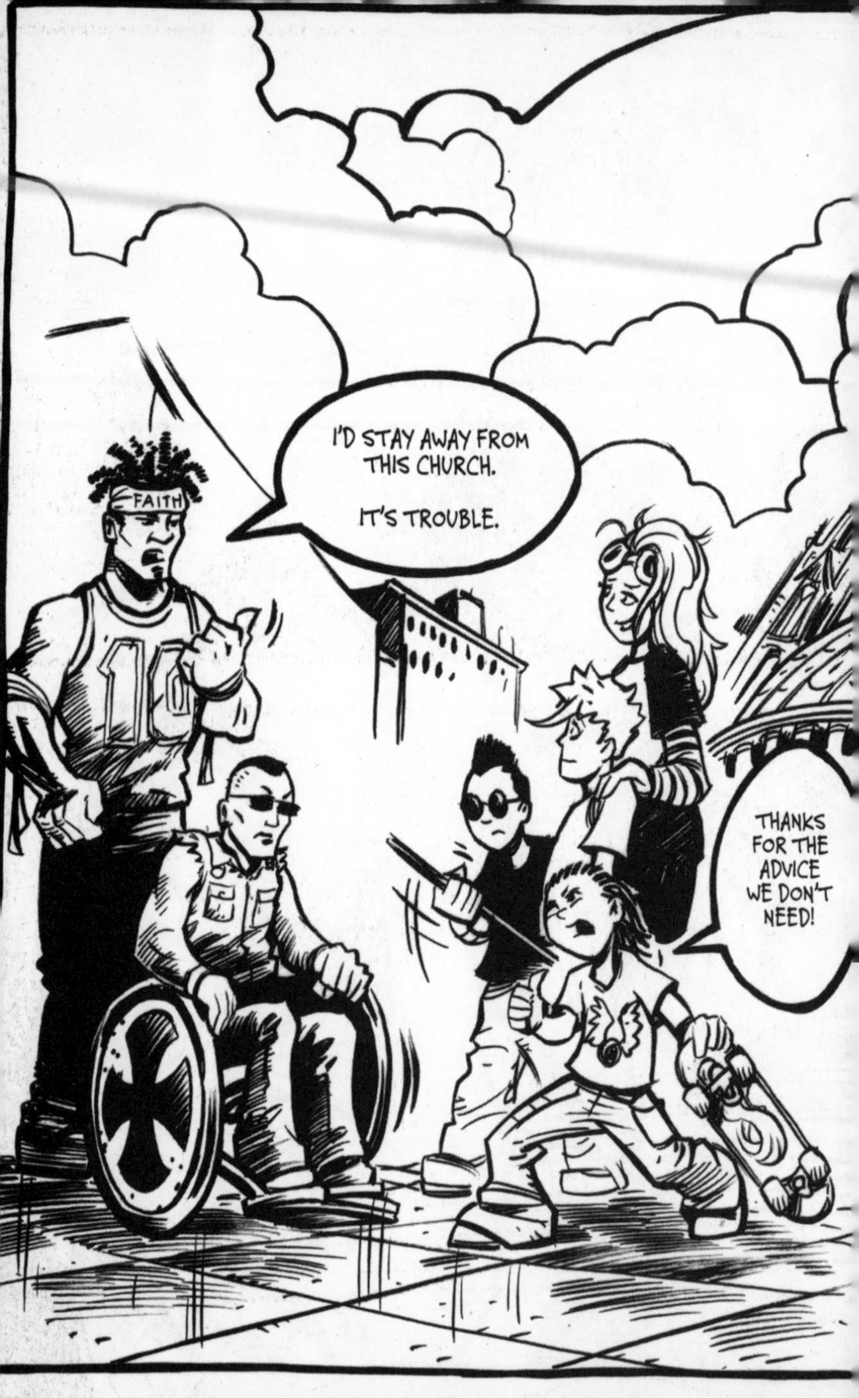
FAITH
I'D STAY AWAY FROM THIS CHURCH.
IT'S TROUBLE.
THANKS FOR THE ADVICE WE DON'T NEED!

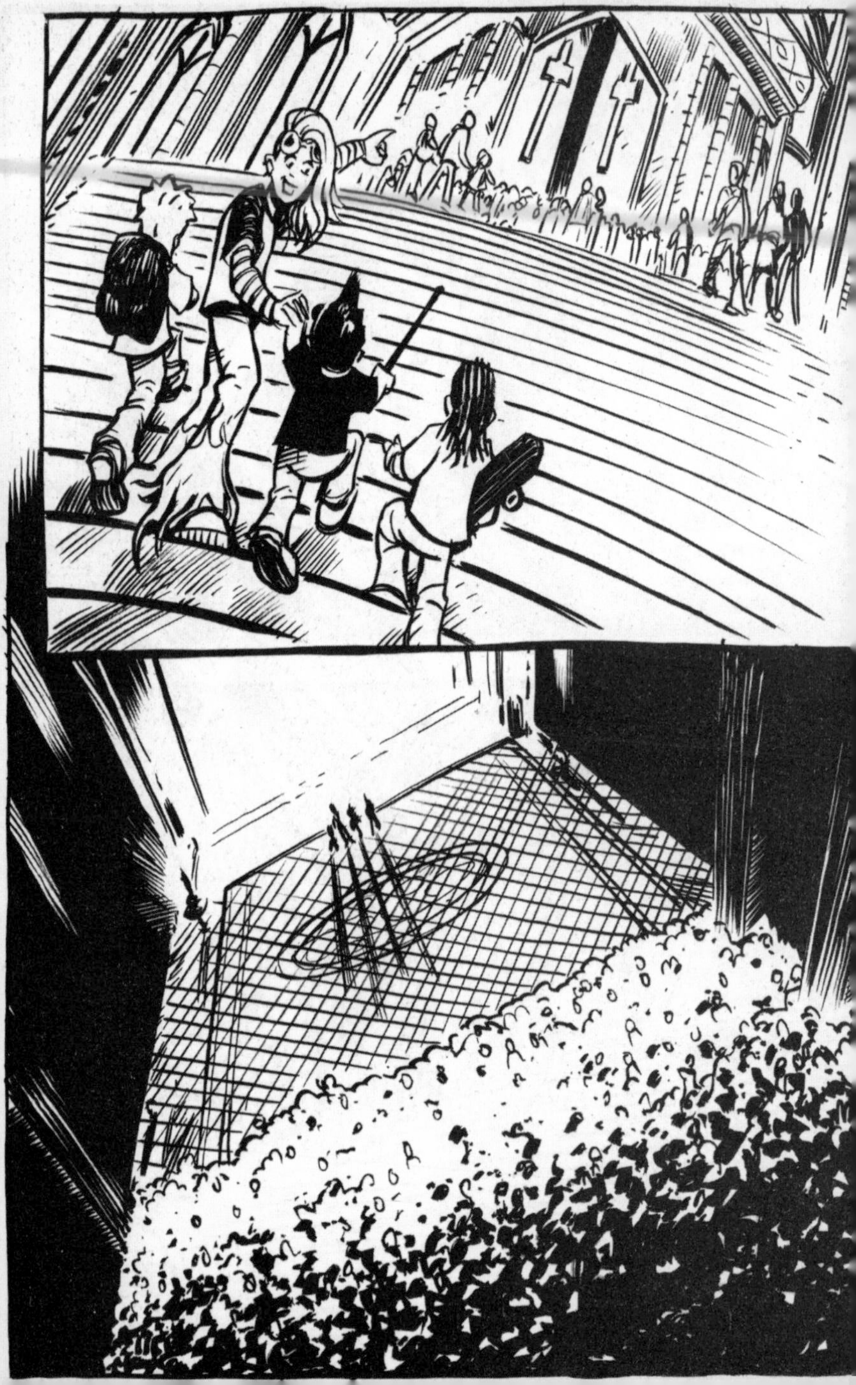

WHOA AGAIN!

LIGHT HOUSE
ORPHANAGE

PLEASE COME TO MEET THE ELDER OF THE CHURCH. I COULD ONLY BRING YOU.
ELDER SEIKO IS A GREAT MAN.

SHOO

ONCE ELDER SEIKO PRAYS OVER YOU, YOU WILL BE DEEPLY TOUCHED.

THIS IS MIA, AN OLD FRIEND OF MINE.

CHILD, MAY I PRAY FOR YOU?
I WOULD BE HONORED ELDER SEIKO.

PASTOR PROMISE, PLEASE HELP ME!

DING
LIL' SMOKER

LIL' SMOKER
ZIP
COUGH COUGH

BAM!
HRRRR
POW
SPLAT!

DING!

WHAT HAPPENED?
GUARDS, CATCH THOSE KIDS THAT ARE COMING OUT OF THE ELEVATOR.
NOW!!!

DING

YAAAHHH

UH OH!

STRIKE!

SKREEE
SWEET!

KRACK
THUNK
TWAP!

FAI
FAITH
BAM

BAP!
FAITH
BAM
BOOF
POP

HMPH!
BIG SMOKER

Cough Cough
THE GATES ARE CLOSING!
I GOT IT!

ZOOOOOOM

BOOM

FAI

UHHH . . .

PLEASE FORGIVE ME FOR NOT HAVING TRUSTED YOU BOTH.
WE WOULDN'T TRUST ANYBODY OURSELVES.
AND WE ALWAYS LOVE A GOOD FIGHT!

FAITH
THESE ARE THE KIDS WE HAVE BEEN LOOKING FOR. ONCE WE HAVE THEIR SOULS NEW CITY CAN'T BE TURNED.

THEY MUST BE LONG GONE BY NOW, AND WON'T COME BACK.
HA!
YOU ARE MISTAKEN. THE GAMES HAVE ONLY JUST BEGUN AND SOON WE WILL HAVE THEM ALL.

HI GARY. PLEASE FORGIVE ME. I'M AFRAID OF NOT SEEING YOU ANYMORE.
MOM! I THOUGHT YOU WERE DEAD! I CAN'T FIND MIA. SHE'S MISSIN I'LL FIND HER, I PROMISE. AND WE'LL ALL BE RE-UNITED!

DELI

DEAR GOD, I THANK YOU FOR MY NEW FRIENDS. I FEEL REBORN AND NOT IN FEAR OF THE WORLD, AS I USED TO.
I BELIEVE THAT I HAVE A CHANCE TO FIGHT EVIL WITH THE TEAM BY MY SIDE.

PLEASE LET MY BROTHER BE SAFE AND SHOW ME WHERE HE COULD BE.

ELDER SEIKO USES THE CHURCH TO ATTRACT INNOCENT FAMILIES TO GET A HOLD OF THEIR KIDS.

IF WE GO BACK IN THERE WE WILL WALK INTO A TRAP.
FAITH
MERCY RISING
THERE HAS TO BE A WAY.
FAITH IS RIGHT, IT'S A TRAP.

I BELIEVE GOD WANTS IT THAT WAY.
I WON'T LET MY BROTHER FALL TO EVIL!
I'M COMING WITH YOU. I'M READY FOR ANYTHING!

ULTRA GLUE GUN
OIL

FAITH

PLAN OF
ATTACK

MASTER SEIKO, EVERYTHING IS READY SIR.
GOOD! KEEP ME INFORMED IF ANYTHING ELSE ARISES.

SMACK
I COULD HAVE TAKEN CARE OF THIS, YOU KNOW.

WE'RE IN. PLAN A READY TO GO.
CHECK.

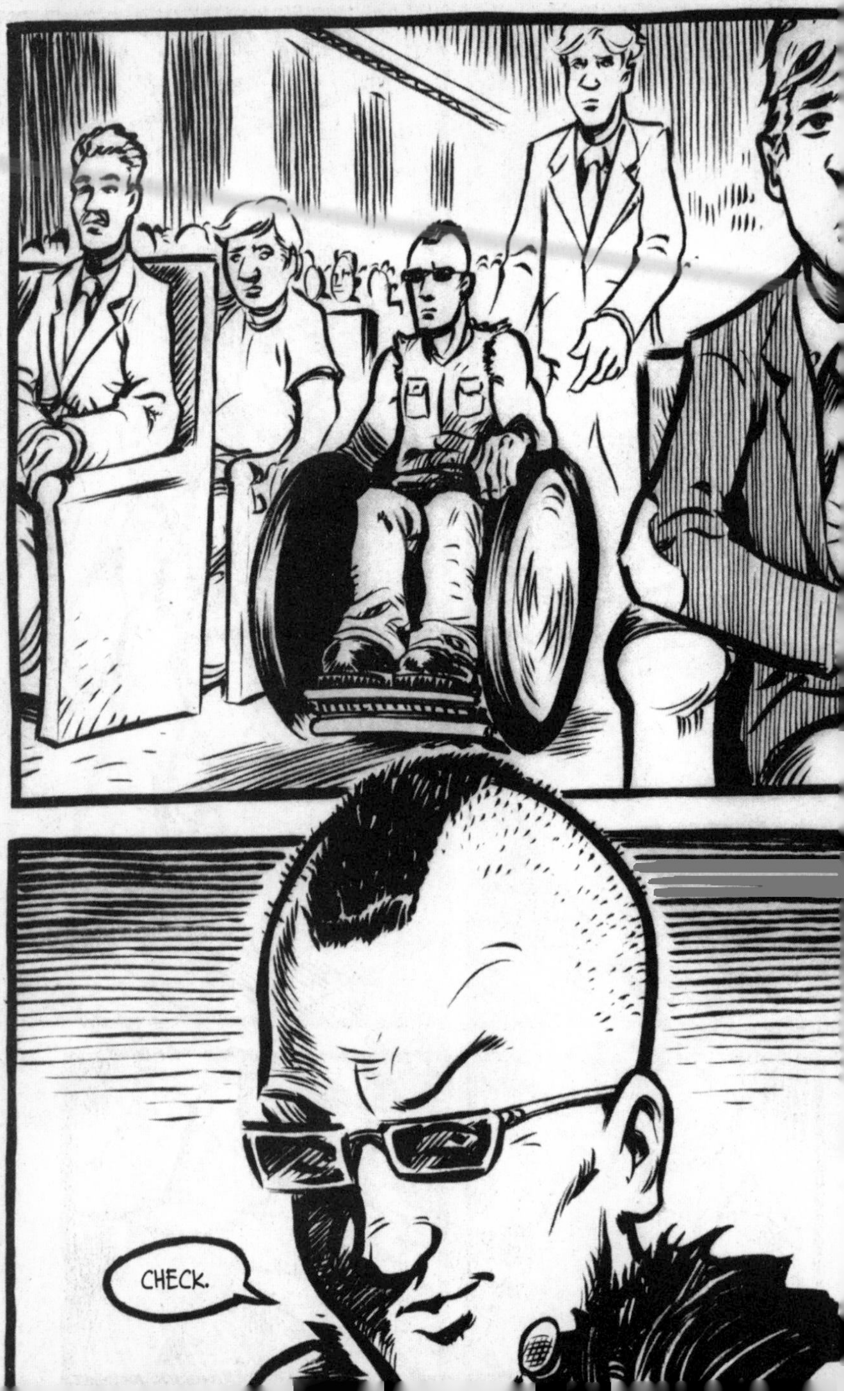
CHECK.

CHECK.

VIDEO
CONTROL

GARY?
GARY?

BEEP
BEEP
WE'RE IN POSITION, READY TO GO.

COPY.
COPY.
COPY.
COPY.
COPY.

IS EVERYBODY IN PLACE? YES.... DEAD OR ALIVE.
GARY
GARY

GARY?

MOM? GARY!
MIA!

MIA?
MIA'S MISSING AND NOT ANSWERING HER COMMUNICATOR.

CONTINUE TO EXECUTE THE PLAN. WE'RE GOING TO TRY TO FIND HER.

I THOUGHT I'D NEVER SEE YOU AGAIN!

THEY'VE RECOGNIZED ME.
I'VE LEFT MY POST SO I DON'T MESS UP THE PLAN.
VIDEO CONTROL ROOM

COUGH
COUGH
COUGH
COUGH
COUGH

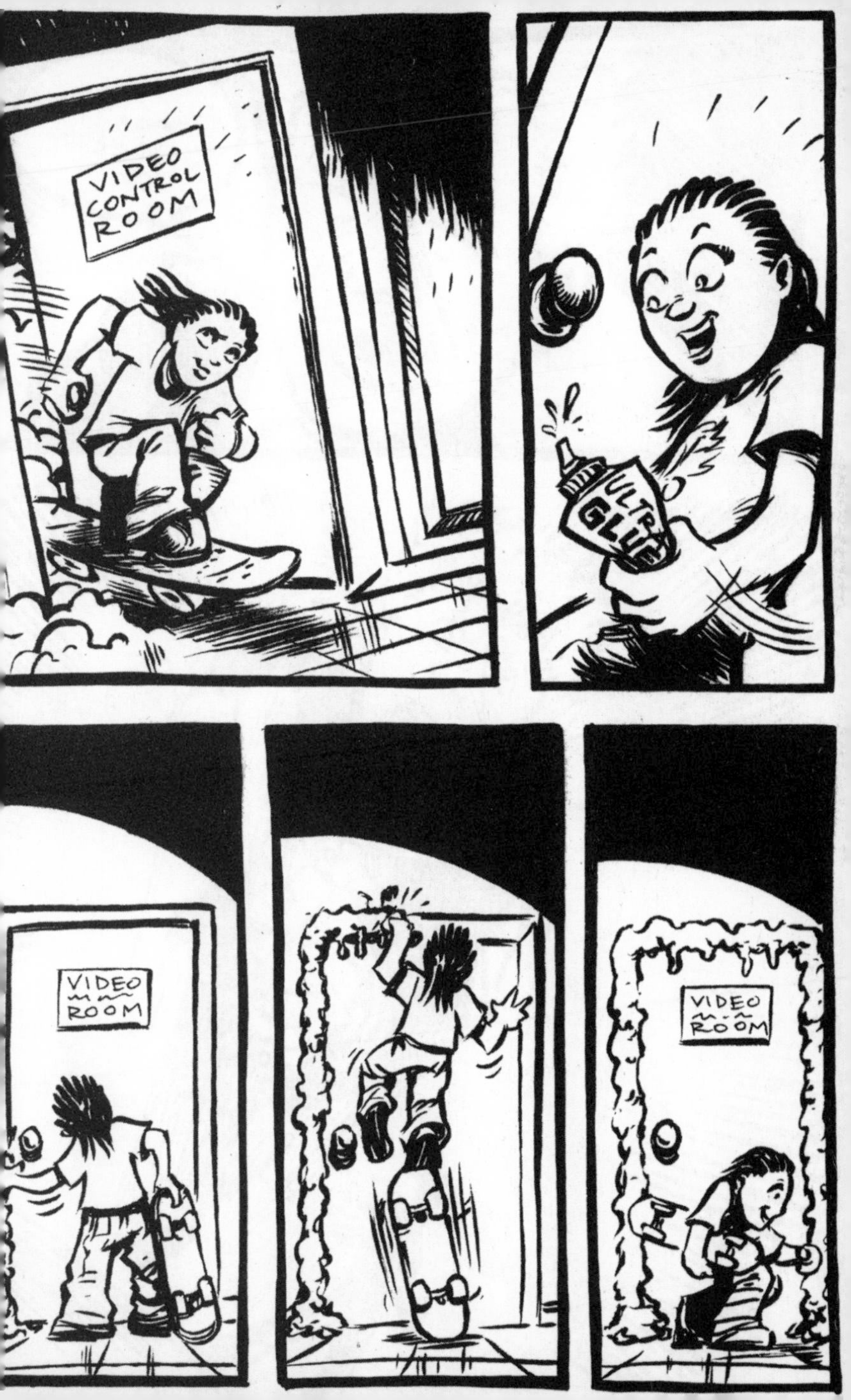
VIDEO CONTROL ROOM
ULTRA GLUE
VIDEO ROOM
VIDEO ROOM

I'VE GOT TO FIND HER.

GARY, DON'T TRUST PASTOR PROMISE. HE HAS TURNED TO EVIL.
YOU'RE WRONG. YOU HAD A BIG MISUNDERSTANDING AND YOUR HEAD KEEPS ON PLAYING TRICKS WITH YOU.

WE DON'T WANT TO HURT YOU, JUST FOLLOW US.

GUYS, TROUBLE IS UNDERWAY. WE'VE ENTERED A TRAP SO LET'S MOVE OUT NOW!
ABORT MISSION . . . I REPEAT, ABORT MISSION

Dear families and friends, we would like to warn you to stay away from this church which has been taken over by evil.

VIDEO CONTROL ROOM

rrrrr...
SHWEW!
WHAM

Your kids are being turned to the dark side by the touch of Elder Seiko.

HELP!
MIA!

BBBDDDDDDDDD

click
click
click
click
SMOKER
LIL' SMOKER

click
click
click
click
click

FATHER IN HEAVEN, PLEASE HELP ME.

IN THE NAME OF JESUS . . .
SATAN, I BIND YOU!

IN THE NAME OF JESUS . . . SATAN, I BIND YOU!

AAHHH
WOOSH
MIA?

NUMBER
TWO

ALSO
AVAILABLE
FROM STEPHEN BALDWIN & livin it
livin it
TESTIMONIES
CHRISTIAN HOSOI
JOSH KASPER
SIERRA FELLERS
LUKE BRADDOCK
PLUS MANY MORE!
BY: STEPHEN BALDWIN
Livin It™: Testimonies
0805443460
9780805443462
livin it
WHAT IT IS
STORIES AND INTERVIEWS WITH
LUKE BRADDOCK
MASON CORNWELL
JAY HAIZLIP
AND MANY OTHERS
STEPHEN BALDWIN
Livin It™: What it is
0805443509
9780805443509
B&H
Available at your favorite retailer or visit:
www.broadmanholman.com
www.livinit.com